"A Tale About a Tail"
Book One in "Mom's Fairy Tales" Series
by Elena Staniv

Editors: Sharon B. Fried and Carolyn D. Sage
Illustrations: Yuliya Lyashun

ISBN-10: 153979959X

ISBN-13: 978-1539799597

A Tale About a Tail

Once upon a time, down under the deep blue sea lived a plain little fish named Moon Glow.

She was very sad, because her tail was too short, or so she thought.

Actually, it really wasn't that short, only a bit shorter than the tails of the other plain fish. It was hardly noticeable, but Moon Glow was sure that everyone was staring at her tail and making fun of it.

One of her friends, Moon Ray, didn't think that Moon Glow's tail was too short at all. He thought it was rather cute. What a shame that Moon Glow didn't realize that. But Moon Ray was too shy to tell her.

Sometimes all of the fish would gather together to dance and play. Moon Glow refused to join them because she was so embarrassed about her tail.

Instead, she would sit at home, all alone, and think of ways to make her tail longer. She performed special exercises every day, and even went on a special diet, but nothing helped!

"Well," thought Moon Glow to herself, "my only hope is to ask the Great Sea Witch for help. After all, if she can turn a Mermaid's tail into legs, I'm sure she can make my tail longer."

The Great Sea Witch lived far away and Moon Glow's friends had heard some scary stories about her.

"She lives in a cave as dark as a moonless night," said some.

"Uh oh," said a very scared Moon Glow. But she wasn't going to let that stop her.

"A terrible dragon protects the entrance to the Great Sea Witch's cave," said others. "He spits fire and destroys everything that crosses his path!"

"Uh oh," said a terrified Moon Glow. Shaking, she promised herself she would find a way to get past him.

"And just to get there you must swim across three seas of hunter fish with very sharp teeth. They will catch you and eat you just like that!"

"Uh oh," said a very scared Moon Glow.

And you must also swim around three islands inhabited by fisherman with very strong, tightly woven nets. If you get caught, that will surely be the end of you!"

"Uh oh," said a trembling Moon Glow. But she was determined and began her journey to the Great Sea Witch.

Moon Glow dodged the sharp toothed hunter fish as she crossed the three seas and managed to evade the strong, tightly woven nets of the fisherman. She swam around the three islands.

She had a terrible time, but finally she arrived at some underwater cliffs in a gloomy desolate place, deep under the sea.

Moon Glow found herself all alone. Not one fish to be seen, not one crab crawled along and no seahorses bounced by. Suddenly she heard a sound like thunder in the distance. As she got closer to the sound she discovered it wasn't thunder at all – it was the dragon snoring.

Moon Glow was so happy to see the dragon because it meant she had come to the right place. But it was too early to celebrate. Yes, the dragon might be asleep, but he slept with one eye open. She remained hidden in the shadows, waiting and watching.

Suddenly a little fish raced past her at breakneck speed. No fish would choose to swim so close to the cliffs unless it was trying to escape a sharp-toothed hunter fish.

The dragon saw the little fish headed his way, his other eye flew open and in a flash flames shot out of his mouth. There was nothing left of the little fish, not even its little tail!

Moon Glow trembled with fear in the safety of her hiding place and continued to observe the dragon.

She discovered that from time to time the dragon would close his other eye, if only for a second.

Moon Glow slowly moved closer to the entrance of the cave. When the dragon opened his eye, she was again safely concealed in the shadows of the underwater cliffs. Thanks to her short tail, it was easy for her to remain hidden.

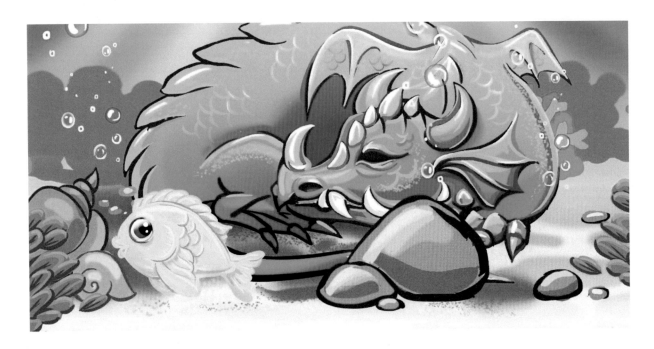

She slowly but surely made her way to the cave's entrance, and at the exact moment when both the dragon's eyes were closed, she sped past him unseen and into the safety of the cave.

Moon Glow swam for hours and hours in total darkness. She bumped into walls and scraped her sides and fins on sharp rocks. She felt lost and desperate to find the Great Sea Witch. She decided to call out to her. After all, what did she have to lose?

"Oh Great Sea Witch, where are you?" shouted Moon Glow at the top of her lungs.

"I'm right here, you silly little thing. Why are you shouting?" asked the Great Sea Witch.

"Is that you, oh Great Sea Witch?" asked Moon Glow.

"Yes, it is!" answered the Great Sea Witch.

"Excuse me, oh Great Sea Witch, but is it possible to turn on the light? It would be nice to be able to see you."

"I'm old and light hurts my eyes, which is why I live in the dark," wheezed the Great Sea Witch, "but I'll allow a small one, just for you."

"Hey, Headlight, turn on your lantern and shine some light over here, please, but don't come too close."

A tiny circle of light appeared not too far away. A funny looking little fish with a lantern on his head swam up to Moon Glow. "Hi! I'm Headlight. Better now?"

"Yes, thank you," nodded Moon Glow, glancing around. Behind her she saw a passage in between the rocks that stuck out like fingers. Those must be the same rocks she'd hurt herself on. Ouch!

Before her, she saw the Great Sea Witch sitting in the middle of a large hall, barely visible in the weak light from Headlight's lantern.

"So," said the Great Sea Witch, "quickly tell me what you came here for. The light is killing my eyes!"

"Can you make my tail longer?" asked Moon Glow in a small voice.

"Why? What's wrong with the one you have?" asked the Great Sea Witch.

"It's very short," sighed Moon Glow, "and short tails aren't pretty."

"Well, I happen to think your tail is quite nice," said the Great Sea Witch, "but if that's what you really want...."

"Yes, it is! Please make my tail longer!" begged Moon Glow.

"What kind of tail would you like?" asked the Great Sea Witch.

"I want a tail just like the Little Mermaid's," said Moon Glow, her heart skipping a beat.

The Great Sea Witch burst out laughing. "Are you kidding? Just look at yourself – you're the size of the Mermaid's little finger. How will you move with a tail that big?"

"So you don't want to give me a new tail then?" pouted Moon Glow.

"You really are a foolish little fish, but have it your way," said the Great Sea Witch. Suddenly Moon Glow felt herself quickly pulled downward, landing with a thump on the sea bed. It's lucky the sea bed is sandy and soft, or she would have crashed to her death.

"So, how do you like your new tail?" asked the Great Sea Witch from above.

"I don't know, I can't move," replied Moon Glow.

"Well, that's no surprise. You've got quite a hefty tail there for a fish your size," said the Great Sea Witch.

"Could you make it just a bit lighter for me, please?" asked Moon Glow.

"Lighter, longer … make up your mind already!" said the Great Sea Witch.

"Long and light, please." said Moon Glow.

"Impossible!" said the Great Sea Witch.

"Then please just make it light enough so that I can move, but do keep it long too," begged Moon Glow.

"Enough already!   Here you go.   And this is final!" said the frustrated Great Sea Witch.

Moon Glow felt the enormous weight lift and she slowly swam up to Headlight who was impatiently scurrying around some distance from the Great Sea Witch.

"Well, what do you think?" whispered Moon Glow. "Isn't it beautiful?"

"Amazing," whispered Headlight. "But …."

Moon Glow wasn't listening. Even in the dim light she could see that the Great Sea Witch had given her a magnificent and beautiful very, very long and elegant tail.

"Thank you, thank you," babbled Moon Glow in utter delight.

"You're welcome, you foolish little fish," snorted the Great Sea Witch. "And now, if you're satisfied, it's time for you to leave. Headlight, turn off your lantern — my eyes can't stand the light anymore! And show her the way out so that she doesn't get lost."

The Great Sea Witch's voice was getting sleepy and as soon as Headlight switched off his lantern, they heard her snoring. "Let's go," he said quietly to Moon Glow.

Suddenly they heard her shout after them, "I know how precious your new tail is to you, Moon Glow, but if one day someone or something else should become more precious to you, then just say 'Return mine, take back thine' and you will have your old tail back."

"Well, that's never going to happen," laughed Moon Glow. "I'm never going to part with my brand new, beloved tail!"

"Whatever," grumbled the Great Sea Witch, and she promptly resumed her obnoxious snoring.

Headlight, who was waiting impatiently, quietly switched on his lantern and raced into a narrow, winding passage leading out of the cave. Moon Glow started to race after him, but found she couldn't move.

"Come on already," called out Headlight.

"I can't," whimpered Moon Glow. "I'm stuck."

"Good grief," grumbled Headlight. "The Great Sea Witch was right when she called you foolish. Come on, I'll give you a push." Getting behind her, he started to push as hard as he could.

"Careful," cried out Moon Glow, "or you'll bend my tail!"

"Really! Your precious tail is going to get in the way everywhere you go!" Headlight sounded pretty angry by now.

"No pain, no gain. Sometimes it's hard to be beautiful," answered Moon Glow proudly.

Headlight sighed. Such a vain little fish, he thought to himself. Ignoring her frightened shrieks, he pushed and pulled Moon Glow all the way to the entrance of the cave.

But getting out of the cave wasn't going to be easy. The dragon wasn't about to let her pass by safely, just because she had a brand new tail!

"What are you going to do?" asked Headlight.

"I'll slip by somehow." Moon Glow really believed the worst was behind her. Headlight couldn't agree more. That large, heavy tail was the worst makeover he had ever seen!

Headlight shook his head. "Not with a tail as big as yours. Listen up - I'll try to distract the dragon while you swim by as fast as you can." He boldly swam out to face the dragon, who was shocked by the daring of this little fish.

He roared and was about to roast him when suddenly Headlight did a somersault and then spun around like a fiery pinwheel. "Welcome to the circus," he proclaimed. "This is our final tour. This evening we present to you our best clown and acrobat performance!"

"What's that?" asked the confused dragon, who had probably never been to a circus in his life.

Headlight dazzled him! He did more somersaults, shot straight up like a rocket and plummeted back down as if falling to his death. His lantern drew mesmerizing patterns as it swung through the water. He mimicked the mean-looking hunter fish.

The dragon was so amazed by Headlight's performance that he began to laugh from pure enjoyment.

He laughed so hard that tears started flowing out of his eyes, and of course he didn't notice when Moon Glow swam out of hiding with her long tail, right under his nose.

She quickly hid in the shadows of the underwater cliffs.

The dragon was exhausted from all that laughing, so Headlight turned off his lantern and quickly joined her. He hardly had a chance to catch his breath when a dark shadow appeared nearby.

"Careful," whispered Headlight.

"Don't worry," Moon Glow whispered back, "he won't see us here in the shadows of the cliffs."

But she was wrong. Her precious long tail stuck out like a sore thumb, letting the hunter fish know that something tasty was hiding there.

And without hesitation, the hunter fish went in for the kill.

"Eeeek!" screamed Moon Glow in horror, but it was too late.

Massive jaws were open and about to eat her up when suddenly a small brave fish came out of nowhere, hurled itself at the hunter fish and pierced its eye.

The hunter fish shook his head around in pain, allowing Moon Glow to make her escape from the terrifying teeth and hide deeper under the cliff.

The confused and hurting hunter fish quickly swam away.

Headlight was just as surprised by the hunter fish, who shamefully disappeared, as he was at the appearance of the heroic little fish who saved their lives.

"Wicked!" exclaimed Headlight, unable to contain his amazement. "Simply wicked! And who are you?"

"My name is Moon Ray," answered the heroic fish humbly.

"Moon Ray?" said Moon Glow sticking her nose out from behind the cliff. "What are you doing here?"

"Well," said an embarrassed Moon Ray, "I was just out for a little swim ...."

"A little swim," said Moon Glow in a knowing tone of voice. "You're a little far from home, aren't you?"

"Ungrateful girl," cried an annoyed Headlight, "he just saved your life and you're making fun of him?"

"Don't listen to her," exclaimed Headlight, as he turned to face Moon Ray. "In fact, just ignore her! This is all because of her ridiculous obsession about needing a longer tail.

And, although it is very beautiful, it is very impractical, and especially for a fish her size!

The only place for her now is in an aquarium. She won't last long in the ocean, that's for sure. Hey, are you listening to me?"

No, Moon Ray wasn't listening. He was staring at Moon Glow, as if seeing her for the first time.

"You are so beautiful," whispered Moon Ray to Moon Glow."

Moon Glow flirtatiously curved her body and swished her new elegant tail for Moon Ray to see in its full glory.

"Aha, he must be in love with the silly girl. I'll leave them alone for a bit," Headlight said to himself.

But there was no time, because the hunter fish, who was probably ashamed of letting a tiny fish scare him away, had returned. He had a menacing look on his face and was obviously determined not to let dinner escape a second time.

"Let's get out of here," shouted Moon Ray. He darted into a narrow opening in the cliffs, pulling Moon Glow behind him.

Headlight raced after them. The hunter fish poked at the rocks with its nose but it couldn't get into the narrow crack. Moon Ray led the way forward, his companions swimming behind him.

"Wait, wait up!" shouted Moon Glow, out of breath. "My tail got tangled up."

"I knew that would happen," grumbled Headlight who was swimming behind her. "That tail is nothing but trouble!"

"Stop your grumbling." said Moon Ray, standing up for the silly fish and her new tail. "Such beauty is worth the trouble that comes with it."

"Thank you," said Moon Glow in a quiet voice. "You're a real friend. But you, what are you still doing here?" she said turning to Headlight. "You can go back to your cave if you don't like my tail!"

"Well there you have it," said Headlight obviously offended. "It's time for me to go home!" He turned around and started swimming in the direction of the cave, but he didn't get far. The hunter fish was waiting for him on the other side of the cliff, still hoping for dinner.

Headlight froze. Swimming forward would lead him straight into sharp-toothed jaws, but he didn't want to swim back either.

Moon Glow had really offended him. He had risked his life to protect her and the silly little fish hadn't even thanked him.

"Don't be offended," said Moon Ray who suddenly appeared beside him. "I know she can be a little demanding at times, but she really is a nice girl."

Headlight shook his head in dismay.

"Please stay with us just a little while longer. We can't manage without you! We've still got a long way to go, the journey is dangerous and on top of that there's the matter of the tail ...."

"But you said it was a good tail," sneered Headlight.

"Not good, beautiful," Moon Ray corrected him.

"Isn't that the same thing?" asked Headlight.

"It depends," answered Moon Ray vaguely. "So, are you coming with us?"

"Okay, I'll give it another try," said Headlight.

They swam back to Moon Glow who had managed to untangle her tail. She looked at them expectantly.

"Tell him you're sorry," said Moon Ray. "I saw how Headlight did somersaults in front of the dragon to protect you. You owe him an apology."

Moon Glow lowered her eyes. She knew she behaved badly, but it was hard for her to apologize.

Moon Ray looked at her sternly. She sighed and mumbled, "I'm sorry, Headlight. Please forgive me. Thank you for everything you did for me."

"Apology accepted," said Headlight. "Let's head out."

And off they went. The going was tough. Moon Glow's elegant tail was constantly getting tangled up in seaweed or stuck in between rocks. On top of that, they were always dodging hunter fish as they searched for food. They made very little progress even though they'd been swimming for hours. Suddenly they came upon the islands that were inhabited by the fisherman with the strong tightly woven nets. Moon Ray and Headlight swam quickly and evaded the nets, but Moon Glow swam slower because of her new long tail, and got caught in one of the nets.

Her friends became frantic, not knowing what to do. Moon Ray moaned with grief, wishing he had sharp teeth to saw through the net so Moon Glow could escape. What was he going to do?

Suddenly Headlight dove down to the ocean floor and began rummaging around, searching by the light of his lantern. "Quick, take this!" he said to Moon Ray.

"What is it? What did you find?" asked Moon Ray as he raced downwards. Headlight was already heading towards him with a razor sharp rock in his mouth.

Moon Ray took the rock and swam swiftly to the net where Moon Glow was trapped, flapping around, trying to escape.

"Start cutting right here," Headlight said urgently, shining his lantern on the exact spot where he wanted Moon Ray to cut.

As Moon Ray furiously cut at the net, Headlight pulled and pulled on the thick cords of rope with all of his might.

At first it seemed fruitless, but finally their hard earned efforts were rewarded. Moon Glow slipped out of the net through the small hole they made and was free to continue on the journey home.

But poor Moon Ray was exhausted. His mouth was torn and bleeding from the razor sharp stone he had used to free Moon Glow. Suddenly he lost consciousness and slowly sank to the sea bed.

Headlight and Moon Glow swam around him frantically as the blood turned the water red. Hunter fish can smell blood from miles away and they both knew that it wouldn't be long before they showed up to claim their prey.

Almost before they finished this thought, the terrifying shadow of a hunter fish started circling closely overhead. Without thinking, Headlight shouted, threw himself in the path of the hunter fish and blinded him temporarily with his lantern.

But he was too small to stop this dangerous enemy for more than a few minutes.

"Stay out of my way, small fry, or you'll be next!" roared the hunter fish, knocking Headlight aside with one effortless flick of his nose.

But Headlight wasn't about to give up. He yelled to Moon Glow to drag Moon Ray behind some rocks while he faced the hunter fish alone, distracting him by dancing around in front of him.

The hunter fish was really angry now and tried to catch Headlight in his sharp jaws, but it was impossible for him to catch such a tiny fish.

Moon Glow had been frozen in fear, but she quickly snapped out

of it and dragged Moon Ray to a narrow opening in between some

rocks.

She started to push him in but his limp body wouldn't cooperate.

Moon Glow tried to swim into the gap first so that she could pull Moon

Ray to safety but her magnificent new tail got in the way.

"I wish you would disappear, you useless tail!" cried Moon Glow

in despair.

Suddenly she remembered the Great Sea Witch's parting words.

"Return mine, take back thine," she shouted at the top of her lungs.

Her new tail immediately fell off and her old tail grew back, allowing Moon Glow to help her friend to safety between the rocks.

And just in time. Headlight was by now too exhausted to continue to distract the hunter fish. He turned off his lantern and hid himself in the sea bed.

The angry hunter fish continued circling a little longer, but soon gave up and left to find easier prey.

More hunter fish came, attracted by the blood, but finding nothing, they gave up and swam away.

Silence descended on the ocean floor.

After a while, a spot in the sea bed started to move.

It was Headlight, checking to see if it was safe to come out. He left his hiding place, turned on his lantern and swam over to his friends, who were too scared to move from their safe spot between the rocks.

The bleeding had stopped and Moon Ray had regained consciousness. Moon Glow was beside him, crying softly, tears pouring down her face. Moon Ray comforted her weakly with one of his fins.

Headlight sighed when he saw Moon Glow had her short tail back. He silently sat down beside them.

"Well, I guess we should head for home," Moon Glow said quietly.

"Wait," said Headlight. "Don't you want to go back to the Great Sea Witch and ask for another tail?"

"No," said Moon Glow. "I've got far more important things to take care of. Moon Ray, as you know, is very weak. We'll swim home slowly, and I'll take care of him until he has recovered from his wounds. I hope you will come visit us some day. Will you be able to find the way?"

"I will," answered Headlight. "Will you manage by yourself?"

"Of course! With my old tail back, I can do anything!" said Moon Glow.

"Thank you so much for all of your help. And I will never forget how brave you were!"

"It was nothing" said an embarrassed Headlight. "I'm just glad you're not upset about your tail."

Moon Glow started laughing. "Are you alright?" asked Headlight.

"I was just picturing myself hiding among the rocks with my tail sticking out. I must have looked so stupid!" said Moon Glow with a wry grin.

And they all laughed together before they parted ways.

Deep down under the ocean, the Great Sea Witch still sleeps away most of her days, always snoring slightly.

She wakes from time to time, stares into the darkness and, feeling bored and lonely, calls for Headlight. They drink tea together and talk of times gone by.

"Do you remember the little fish who came here to ask for a longer tail?" asked the Great Sea Witch.

"I remember," answered Headlight. "How could I forget such a silly fish? And in the end, she took her old tail back."

The Great Sea Witch laughed but said nothing. Headlight remembered every detail. "She went to so much trouble and in the end it was all for nothing." He shook his lantern as he sipped his tea.

"You don't say," responded the Great Sea Witch. "Do you really think it was all for nothing?"

Thank you for reading "A Tale About a Tail"
If you enjoyed reading this book,
please leave a review on Amazon.com

For updates on new releases and to receive special bonuses
and discounts, sign up on Elena Staniv's mailing list by
visiting her website at www.staniv.com

"The Little Wizard"!
Book Two in "Mom's Fairy Tales" Series

can also be found on Amazon.com
and on CreateSpace eStore
Don't miss it!

I am offering my readers 10% off the purchase price
with Discount Code CUAKW36Q
Enjoy!

41780713R00024

Made in the USA
Middletown, DE
22 March 2017